The
Chicken
Knitters

By **Cath Jones**

Illustrated by
Sean Longcroft

Chapter 1

Clickety-click-click. Lilly was busy knitting in her bedroom. Suddenly, she heard a strange noise coming in through her open window. CLUCK-SOB-SIGH.

It was coming from Old Barn Farm at the end of the road.

Lilly had heard about Farmer Claw's chicken farm. He didn't care if his hens were happy or not. Eggs, eggs, eggs: that was all that mattered.

Lilly wondered if the strange sound might be coming from some unhappy hens. She tucked her knitting needles behind her ears and grabbed her enormous knitting bag. She had to find out.

The barn door was locked but that didn't stop Lilly. She poked a knitting needle into the lock. Clickety-click-click, the door swung open. Lilly gasped. Hundreds of chickens were crammed into the barn and they had hardly any feathers!

"Hello girls," she whispered sadly. "Has Farmer Claw not been looking after you properly?"

The chickens gazed up at her with unhappy eyes.

"Chin up, chickens," Lilly said. "I'm here to help."

She popped open her big bag and quick as a flash, three chickens dashed over and

climbed in. Dozens more chickens darted out through the door. Every evening, Lilly tiptoed back to the barn and rescued more chickens. By the weekend, Farmer Claw was hopping mad.

"Where are my chickens?" he roared. He stamped his feet, gnashed his teeth and jumped up and down! "Just you wait until I catch you," he yelled, "you chicken thieving gangsters." He slammed shut the big barn door and... CLINK!

A knitting needle fell out of the lock. Farmer Claw stared at it suspiciously.

Chapter 2

Lilly gazed round her bedroom. There were chickens everywhere!

She gave each one a name. Ginger nested under the bed, Gloria settled on top of the wardrobe and Gladys snoozed in Lilly's sock drawer.

"Brrrrrrr!" Gloria shivered.

"Oh!" said Lilly. "You must be chilly without feathers." She picked up some knitting needles and began to make cosy chicken-sized jumpers.

The chickens listened to the clickety-click-clicking of Lilly's knitting needles. They chased balls of wool around the room. They pecked at strands of wool and clucked happily.

Suddenly there was a loud knocking on the front door.

"Hoy!" yelled an unfriendly voice. "Have you seen any chickens?"

The hens began to squawk in panic.

Lilly tucked her knitting needles behind her ears and popped her head out of the window.

"Good morning, Farmer Claw," she called down in a friendly voice.

He stared at her suspiciously. "Did I hear clucking?" he said.

"Must be on the television," Lilly laughed. "Good luck with finding your chickens. Goodbye!"

She slammed the window shut and turned around.

"Agh!" Lilly tripped over a chicken. She toppled onto the bed.

SPLAT!

"Oops!"

She'd landed on an egg!

"There are too many of you crammed into my tiny bedroom," declared Lilly. "You're safe and warm here, but is it really any better than being in the barn? I need to find you chickens the perfect place to live!"

"You need your own homes, with room to run about and green grass to peck," she said.

No sooner had Lilly said this than an idea popped into her head. She knew the perfect place.

Chapter 3

That afternoon, Lilly put on her pink wellington boots and spotty raincoat.

"Girls!" she called to the chickens. "It's time to go to school."

She picked up her knitting bag and set off down the road. Ginger, Gloria and Gladys dashed after her and all the other chickens followed.

Behind an enormous old oak tree, something rustled. It was Farmer Claw! His eyes nearly popped out of his head when he saw his chickens trotting after Lilly.

He gnash-gnash-gnashed his teeth. "I want my chickens back," he snarled.

Five minutes later, he watched Lilly and the chickens trot into school. He smiled. He had

thought of a plan.

"Hello, Lilly!" the children called, and they waved excitedly at the chickens. "You're just in time to join in with knitting club!"

The chickens settled down with happy clucks. They listened to the click-click-clicking of the knitting and peered and pecked at the needles.

"I need your help," Lilly said. "The girls lost their feathers in Farmer Claw's chicken barn. They are feeling a little bit chilly."

"Brrrrrrr," said the chickens.

"Can you help knit some more cosy chicken-jumpers?" asked Lilly.

The champion knitters of the knitting club got cracking straight away.

After a while, Ginger and Gladys grabbed knitting needles and Gloria tugged at some wool. Lilly watched in shock as Ginger, Gladys and Gloria began to knit! Soon all the chickens were joining in too.

No one noticed Farmer Claw sneaking through the school gates.

Chapter 4

A little while later, Lilly gazed happily at the chickens.

"You look so cosy in your warm woolly jumpers!" she said. "Now, all we need to do is find the perfect home for you!"

The chickens clucked in agreement and carried on knitting.

Lilly set off to see
Edna McClusky,
the school
caretaker. Perhaps
Edna could help.

Edna listened carefully
to the story of how the
chickens escaped. Then
she nodded, and reached
for her hammer and
some nails.

Soon, the school echoed with the sound of
hammering. Edna and Lilly built dozens of
wooden hen houses.

They placed them around the school garden and Lilly painted the names of the chickens on the front of each house.

Deep in the bushes, Farmer Claw watched. He gnashed his teeth furiously. "My chickens belong at Old Barn Farm," he snarled.

CLUMP-CLUMP-CLUMP went his boots on the soft grass as he crept closer to the chickens.

"Girls!" called Lilly. She showed them their new homes. Ginger, Gloria and Gladys danced with delight.

Lilly sighed happily at the sound of the joyful

clucks. Finally, the girls had cosy homes with space to run about and plants to peck. They were safe and warm!

CLUMP-CLUMP-CLUMP.

Lilly froze. Her eyes opened wide.

"Eek!" she shrieked.

The chickens clucked nervously at the mysterious figure sneaking out of the bushes.

"Look out!" whispered Lilly. "Farmer Claw knows we're here!"

Lilly quickly rounded up all the chickens. Something had to be done. They had to stop Farmer Claw.

"Let's hatch a plan!" Lilly said.

Chapter 5

Lilly and the chickens knitted for ages. Soon the hen houses were overflowing with strange looking knitting. They were almost ready to put their plan into action.

Farmer Claw waited until all was quiet then he stole out of the bushes. It was time to make his move.

CLUMP-CLUMP-CLUMP.

He carried a great, big sack over his shoulder. "Time to come back to Old Barn Farm," he snarled.

He opened the door of Ginger's hen house and reached inside.

Ginger pounced with her claws!

"EEK!" yelled Farmer Claw.

Gladys was waiting too. She flapped her wings in Farmer Claw's face while Gloria leapt out and pecked his big bottom.

"Agghh!" Farmer Claw let out a roar. He dropped his sack and tried to run away.

But Lilly and the knitting club were ready. So were the chickens... and so was Edna McClusky.

It was time to use their knitted Farmer Claw trap!

BOING! A giant knitted net sprang into the air.

WHI-I-I-I-ZZ! A tangle of knitting whizzed from the windows.

WHOOSH! Balls of wool shot out from the hen houses.

Farmer Claw tumbled to the ground and the chickens pounced. They wound knitting around his head. They wrapped wool around his arms and Lilly tied Farmer Claw's hands

behind his back.

Farmer Claw staggered up off the ground and fled. The chickens chased him all the way back to Old Barn Farm.

"I've had enough of chickens," wailed Farmer Claw. "You can have Old Barn Farm. I'm off!"

Lilly and the chickens never ever saw Farmer Claw again. They turned Old Barn Farm into the Knitting Barn. Chickens travelled from far and wide to get their very own, cosy chicken jumpers. Lilly and the girls became the most famous knitters in the world!

The End

Book Bands for Guided Reading

The Institute of Education book banding system is a scale of colours that reflects the various levels of reading difficulty. The bands are assigned by taking into account the content, the language style, the layout and phonics. Word, phrase and sentence level work is also taken into consideration.

Maverick Early Readers are a bright, attractive range of books covering the pink to white bands. All of these books have been book banded for guided reading to the industry standard and edited by a leading educational consultant.

To view the whole Maverick Readers scheme, visit our website at
www.maverickearlyreaders.com

Or scan the QR code above to view our scheme instantly!